ISBN 0-14-100251-4

9 780141 002514

900000

EAN

~ Elizabeth ~

BLESS THIS
HOUSE

ANNE LAUREL CARTER

PQA688991

OUR
CANADIAN
Girl

Elizabeth
BLESS THIS
HOUSE

ANNE LAUREL CARTER

Elizabeth
BLESS THIS
HOUSE

ANNE LAUREL CARTER

Penguin Books

PENGUIN BOOKS

Published by the Penguin Group

Penguin Books Canada Ltd, 10 Alcorn Avenue, Toronto, Ontario, Canada M4V 3B2

Penguin Books Ltd, 80 Strand, London WC2R 0RL, England

Penguin Putnam Inc., 375 Hudson Street, New York, New York 10014, U.S.A.

Penguin Books Australia Ltd, 250 Camberwell Road, Camberwell, Victoria 3124, Australia

Penguin Books (NZ) Ltd, cnr Rosedale and Airborne Roads, Albany, Auckland 1310, New Zealand

Penguin Books Ltd, Registered Offices: Harmondsworth, Middlesex, England

DESIGN: MATTHEWS COMMUNICATIONS DESIGN INC.

MAP ILLUSTRATION: SHARON MATTHEWS

INTERIOR ILLUSTRATIONS: JAMES BENTLEY

First published, 2002

3   5   7   9   10   8   6   4   2

Manufactured in Canada

NATIONAL LIBRARY OF CANADA CATALOGUING IN PUBLICATION DATA

Carter, Anne, 1953–

Bless this house : Elizabeth

(Our Canadian girl)

ISBN 0-14-100251-4

1. Acadians—Expulsion, 1755—Juvenile fiction.
2. New Englanders—Nova Scotia—History—18th century—Juvenile fiction.
I. Title. II. Series.

PS8555.A7727B58 2002   jC813'.54   C2001-902667-6

PZ7.C2427Bl 2002

Visit Penguin Canada's website at **www.penguin.ca**

For
Kaitlyn

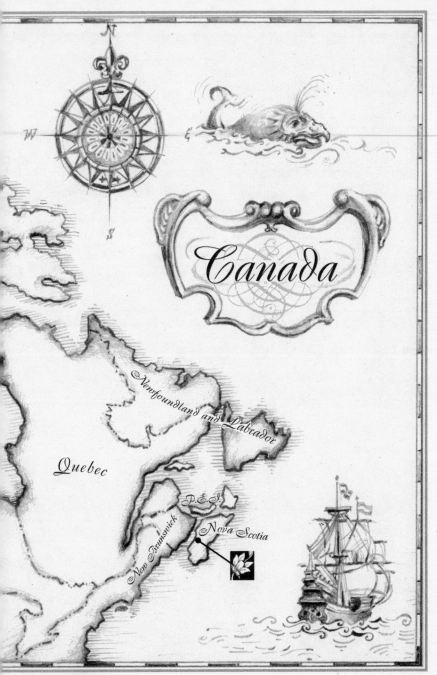

Canada

Newfoundland and Labrador

Quebec

P.E.I.

New Brunswick

Nova Scotia

 Marks the location of the story

MEET ELIZABETH

FOR ONE HUNDRED AND FIFTY YEARS NOVA SCOTIA was "Acadia" to thousands of French-speaking, Catholic farmers. The Acadians led a quiet, independent life farming the rich marshlands around the Bay of Fundy until 1755, just before the Seven Years' War erupted between England and France.

At the time, Acadia was an English colony, ruled by an aggressive military governor in Halifax. With England and France at war, the governor decided to get rid of the Acadians, even though they were peaceful people—known as the French Neutrals— who didn't take sides. He confiscated their lands, burned their farms, and deported nearly ten thousand men, women, and children, sending them to their fate with a strong message: never come back.

By 1756 the English and French were pitted against

each other in the Seven Years' War. Meanwhile, the Acadians survived as poor refugees in English colonies on the eastern seaboard. They had one hope: somehow, someday to return home.

Meanwhile, the governor in Halifax had plans for their confiscated lands. He sent land agents to New England to entice English Protestant settlers, who are known as "Planters"—those who "planted" colonies—to come to Nova Scotia. They were offered free passage, plenty of cheap land, and all the help they needed. The Planters began arriving from Massachusetts, Connecticut, Rhode Island, and Maine in 1761 and 1762. They were mostly Congregationalists: good, hard-working people with strong beliefs in God and democracy.

Elizabeth Brightman was born in Connecticut. In 1762 her Congregationalist father and mother decided to immigrate to Nova Scotia—the last thing in the world Elizabeth wanted to do. But in those days, no one listened to a ten-year-old girl.

Elizabeth couldn't change laws or politics in the adult world around her. But she had a strong sense of right and wrong and a kind heart. Face to face with a difficult situation in Nova Scotia, she knew she would have to speak out for what she felt was right.

CHAPTER 1

"Don't let him have our farm!" Elizabeth tugged on her father's sleeve.

"We'll need the money in Nova Scotia," Papa answered gently.

They stood at the window with Mama, watching the stranger walk up their road, an enormous man with a broad sea captain's hat.

Leaving. The thought made Elizabeth squirm. It felt worse than having to attend Sunday meeting in wet woollen stockings. How much better to rip them off and *stay home*. If only they could!

But it was too late. Papa was leaving tomorrow with the men; she and Mama would follow in June. And here was the sea captain who was interested in buying their farm.

If only that land agent had never come, never convinced the Worths or her parents or so many of their neighbours to become Planters. Elizabeth knew from her heart to her bare feet it was a bad idea.

She squirmed again. Maybe if she told Mama about her bad dream? In her mind she saw the strange little house on fire. She looked up into her mother's careworn face.

"I had a dream about Nova Scotia. A house was burning—"

"Moving's unsettling," her mother said, patting her hand. "We'll have a fresh start in Nova Scotia, you'll see."

The captain loomed in their doorway, his coat billowing around him like a sail.

Papa nodded politely. "You've come about the farm?"

Before Elizabeth could cry out "Mistake!" the captain swept off his hat and boasted, "I'm the only man in all Connecticut who'd even think of purchasing your pitiful farm!"

Papa stopped smiling. Mama didn't invite the captain in. Behind her the great kettle stayed cold on the stone hearth and the best china teacups sat empty.

"If you're worried about the land's yield—"

"I've no worries whatsoever!" The captain laughed, pushing his way past them into the company room like a tall ship commanding its new harbour. "England's finally silenced those French dogs. This damn war will be over soon."

"I won't deceive you, the land's rocky and—"

"Land!" roared the captain. "What use have I for rocks and trees?" He pointed out the window to the distant harbour. "That's where I make my living. The sea. And we rule it now! So I'll buy your little house, for it means I can find a little wife to sit at this window awaiting my safe return."

He thrust his hairy hand towards Elizabeth and pinched her cheek. Horrified, Elizabeth smacked it away.

"You can't want our house." What could she say to discourage him? "It's . . . cursed."

Papa gave Mama a meaningful look. "Take Elizabeth outside. We'll negotiate in private."

Shawls were gathered and Mama pushed her towards the door.

"A cursed home is it?" The captain laughed greedily. "I'll have to rethink my offer and a fair price—"

The door slammed shut.

Suddenly, everything, the world as she knew it, tumbled inside, outside, all around Elizabeth.

"Fair?" she cried. Hot tears wet her cheeks. "Baby brothers die. Our crops fail . . . Papa's leaving tomorrow, and that horrid man gets our house . . ."

Mama's face softened. "But we don't want it. I share your bad feeling about it."

"No! No! It's moving to Nova Scotia I feel bad

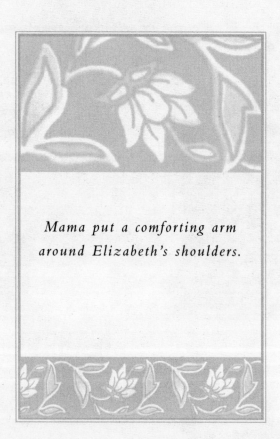

Mama put a comforting arm around Elizabeth's shoulders.

about! I had a terrible dream . . . soldiers, and a fire burning the new house." Elizabeth saw again the tiny log house with a thatched roof . . . nothing like their real home, which had a large front room to entertain company and bedrooms upstairs.

Mama put a comforting arm around Elizabeth's shoulders. They walked slowly past the garden. "We've had years of bad luck. This is a good sign: a buyer for the farm."

All her feelings gathered like a storm cloud and Elizabeth argued, "I hate Rebecca Worth. She got the women to convince you something's wrong with our farm, that you'll never have more children if you stay here. It's her fault we're leaving."

Mama stiffened, and briefly closed her beautiful dark blue eyes. They had reached the far side of the garden, and Elizabeth's words hit a tender spot. In a corner, two wooden crosses marked two small graves covered in a bit of late-March snow.

Elizabeth's first brother had lived just a month. The second had survived only a few short days.

Both brothers were buried there under the willow trees.

Elizabeth found a few stones and placed them on the snowy graves. *Please God,* she prayed. *Tell them we'll always remember.*

Such short lives. Such a long shadow left on their hearts! And the shadow had lengthened. Last summer's crops had rotted in the constant rain. Then the land agent had come, and Rebecca Worth had convinced Mama to leave.

For the first time in months, Mama's voice sounded hopeful.

"God's face will shine upon us in the new land. I know it."

Elizabeth couldn't stay angry for long—not at Mama.

"Maybe God's face is shining on us right now. Maybe . . . there's just a cloud in the way."

Mama laughed at her. "You're just like your Papa."

Elizabeth straightened her shoulders. Yes. She was like Papa. Cheerful. She even looked like him. Straight brown hair. Freckled cheeks.

On the willow branch above the graves Elizabeth noticed a fat, red-breasted robin. It began to chirp its clear and boisterous spring song: *I'm first, I'm first.*

Another sound interrupted. Voices. The sea captain and Papa were shaking hands outside the front door.

It could mean only one thing: the farm was sold.

She would be a Planter, Elizabeth thought. The first to settle the vacant lands. *I'm first. I'm first.*

Mama was right. Of course, the sun had to shine in Nova Scotia too. She would just pack her worries in the bottom of her trunk. The *very* bottom.

Maybe there would be a bright side to this leaving. Maybe, she could hide *all* her unwanted things at the bottom of the trunk? Perhaps . . . her woollen stockings?

CHAPTER N<u>o</u> 2

It rained every day on the long voyage to Nova Scotia. The *Lydia* was like a prison. Sleeping in the dark, cramped hold was miserable, but having nowhere to play was agony. Below deck, the air was damp and foul. By the second day the stench of human and animal waste in the hold had killed Elizabeth's appetite. Whenever the rain let up, Elizabeth rushed on deck, desperate for fresh air and the sky.

Her spirits soared the moment the sloop entered the Bay of Fundy, guns poised. Even the sun appeared, bringing a bit of late-June warmth.

The coastline was just a series of bumps on the horizon. Elizabeth sat slightly apart from the other girls on deck of the *Lydia,* daydreaming. Papa wasn't far now. How she'd missed him! And the cows and pigs! Papa had taken the livestock, leaving only the hens to provide fresh eggs. She couldn't wait to see the new barn, to milk old Bessie and—

"What's on *your* sampler, Elizabeth?"

Sarah Worth interrupted Elizabeth's daydream. Sarah's mother had given the girls linen and coloured thread to make samplers for their new homes. Elizabeth's lay unfinished in her lap and she picked it up guiltily. She hated needlework.

All week she'd struggled through the alphabet on her sampler, counting cross-stitches. Finally she'd reached Z. *Stitchery, fitchery*. She'd never finish the next task: stitching a verse.

"Elizabeth, you must try harder. I've finished my alphabet *and* a verse already," Sarah Worth said. The other girls—Ellen Porter, Maggie, and

Priscilla Young—looked as Sarah held up her sampler.

Elizabeth stared at Sarah Worth. She was the spitting image of her mother: plump cheeks and perfect blond curls that bounced on her shoulders. Only two years older than Elizabeth, Sarah had the annoying confidence of a twelve-year-old grandmother.

"Shall I read it to you?"

Stitchery, fitchery, foo, Elizabeth thought.

Sarah read:

> I sigh not for beauty
> Nor languish for wealth.
> But grant me kind Providence
> Virtue and health.
> Then richer than Kings
> And more happy than they,
> My days will pass sweetly
> And swiftly away.

The other girls clapped. Elizabeth jabbed her

needle into her sampler. She'd lost count of her stitches.

"What's yours say, Maggie?"

Maggie was the youngest, barely nine. "The Lord is my shepherd. I shall not want," she quoted.

This brought more nods until Sarah pointed out, "A good start. But the Twenty-third is a short psalm. You'd do well to stitch more lines lest you appear lazy."

Maggie's smile faded.

Sarah turned to Priscilla, but Priscilla wisely changed the subject. "Is anyone else afraid of the Bay of Fundy? Mama says the Indians in Nova Scotia have strange powers, making the ocean rise and fall fifty feet between tides."

Sarah sniffed. "If they had such great powers, they wouldn't have surrendered to us. My Papa wrote us that Nova Scotia's a land of plenty. Any hard-working, God-fearing family has nothing to fear."

Elizabeth remembered the strange letter Papa had written: "Nova Scotia is very different from

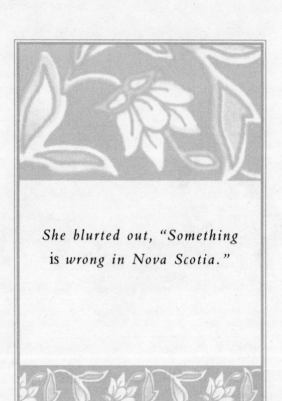

She blurted out, "Something is wrong in Nova Scotia."

Connecticut. Only seven years ago, the French Acadians called it home. That is a sad page in history. The English invite us to settle the vacant lands. There is much work to be done . . ."

Papa's letter had stirred up Elizabeth's uneasiness. If only her worries would stay hidden in the bottom of her trunk!

She blurted out, "Something *is* wrong in Nova Scotia."

Needlework stopped. Eyes turned in astonishment towards Elizabeth.

Maggie gulped. "What makes you say that?"

"I . . . I just know it."

Sarah shook her curls angrily. "You're wrong, Elizabeth Brightman. My Papa is an elder and the best carpenter in all New England. He's going to build many ships in Nova Scotia. He says, 'Those who work together will prosper together.' "

Elizabeth was at a loss for words. How could she explain the terrible dream—soldiers, and the little house on fire? Or the cold dread inside her whenever they mentioned the Acadians?

Sarah pointed at Elizabeth's sampler. "Heed my advice, Elizabeth Brightman, just as your Papa heeds my father who builds your new house. The only thing that's wrong . . . is your sampler!"

Elizabeth looked at her work. She'd finally finished the Z.

The other girls moved closer and stared too. They started to giggle.

Furious, Elizabeth folded her apron over her sampler and jumped to her feet. "You think you know everything. You'll see." She stamped her foot. "You'll see tomorrow when we land."

Sarah stopped smiling. There was a flicker of fear in her wide blue eyes.

Immediately, Elizabeth regretted her words. Why couldn't she be cheerful and get along with Sarah Worth?

In a confusion of emotion, Elizabeth turned and ran to the stern. The sailors were cleaning the great guns. A thick coil of rope sat off to one side, and Elizabeth collapsed behind it, shedding the tears she'd guarded for months. Sarah was right about one thing. Whatever lay ahead, lay ahead for all of them.

Something pricked her arm, bringing her back to her senses. The needle. She unfolded her apron and held out her sampler. What, oh what was wrong with it?

Silently, she read her alphabet, cross-stitched with indigo thread.

A B C D E F G H I K L M N

Foo, foo, foo! She was a ninny for stitching. She would have cried if she hadn't spent all her tears.

Suddenly, she had an idea. She wouldn't pull out her stitches. Her sampler wouldn't be perfect, but Mama and Papa wouldn't mind.

She smiled and began to sew the last letter into her alphabet:

A B C D E F G H I K L M N O P Q R S T
U V W X Y Z . . . J

CHAPTER *N°* 3

Late the following afternoon, the Lydia arrived in the Minas Basin. Everyone crowded on deck, eager to be off the ship. They had to wait for high tide before they could draw close to shore.

In the distance, Elizabeth could see the upper sections of support beams under the wooden wharf, standing in the mud flats like skinny heron legs waiting for the sea-water to rise again.

She stared at the strange shore remembering her dream of the night before. The little house was on fire again. Soldiers chased her, but wherever she ran, there was always another little house on fire. Orange flames. Black smoke. Elizabeth squeezed her eyes shut tight.

Disappear, dream.

She opened her eyes. Around the bay the land lay flat and golden, then rose in hills covered by dense green forest. Up a hill beyond the dock stood the buildings of Fort Edward—not burning—safe.

Elizabeth breathed more easily as men, some of them red-coated soldiers, emerged from the wooden fort, driving carts down the dirt road towards the wharf. A group of children ran behind.

Strange. What children were here? Soldiers were not allowed to bring their families.

Mama hurried her to bundle her belongings and secure the hens in their cage. Finally ready, Elizabeth stared again into the crowd of soldiers and men gathering on the wharf.

"There's Papa," she cried, yanking Mama's sleeve. They laughed, waving at Papa, whose dark head bobbed with excitement at the back of the crowd. And before Elizabeth could say "Connecticut" *or* "Nova Scotia," they were on shore, reunited. Horses neighed. Hens clucked with excitement. In front of everybody, Mama and Papa kissed! Amazed, Elizabeth looked to see if anyone had noticed. But all the adults were doing the same thing. Even Sarah's parents.

"You're a sight for sore eyes," Papa said, swinging Elizabeth off her feet. "And bigger than ever!"

"Where's our new house?" Elizabeth asked, bursting with curiosity. "Is it ready? Is there a barn? Are there any new calves—?"

"All in good time." Papa laughed. Then he looked past her and the smile left his face. "Right now, Captain Mercer wants our attention."

Elizabeth turned around. A stern-looking officer had started speaking to the crowd.

"In the name of his Majesty, George the Third, welcome. Fort Edward is at the service of the Planters."

A cheer went up.

"My soldiers have already helped build several new houses and barns. Until all your homes are ready, some of you will be billeted within the fort." The captain paused. "I regret to announce . . . in the last few weeks . . . we have been forced to accommodate a large number of Acadian prisoners."

Acadians! Fearful cries rose from the women.

Captain Mercer raised his hands for silence. "I understand your fear. But these are destitute families, deported seven years ago to New England, foolishly hoping to return. Of course, the governor in Halifax cannot allow them to live here. Officially we're still at war until France signs a peace treaty with England. They'll be deported again."

Behind them, a cry rose from the young children who had come from the fort. Elizabeth turned to stare. Were they Acadians? They stood at a distance, a thin, ragged, barefoot bunch, listening intently. The oldest in the group was a

fierce-looking girl with black button eyes—
glaring directly at her.

Elizabeth felt accused of an unknown crime
and turned away.

Captain Mercer continued. "I apologize for the
crowded conditions in the fort. I urge those
amongst you who can lodge others to do so."

Now Sarah Worth glared at her too, as if to say
you and your terrible feeling caused this mess. How
unfair.

Everyone began talking at once. Papa said
something to Mama, then moved away to talk to
Caleb Worth.

Mama whispered to Elizabeth, "Papa says the
conditions in the fort are deplorable. Not much
better than on the *Lydia,* if you can imagine!
Thanks to Caleb Worth, our new house is ready.
We must let the Worths and Youngs stay there
until their houses are ready next week. There's an
old house beside it where we'll stay. I can't think
of anything nicer than having them close."

Elizabeth couldn't think of anything *less* nice.

A meeting was called for the following morning to organize reconstruction of the houses they had brought to reassemble here. Then everyone began to gather up belongings.

Please God, Elizabeth prayed, *let them finish Sarah's house first.*

When everything was settled in the cart, Elizabeth sat up front in the warm space between Mama and Papa. They jostled along a dirt road away from the wharf and fort.

Out in the bay the waves danced in a sparkling afternoon sun. Along the shore the marsh grasses rustled in the breeze. Elizabeth felt a glimmer of unexpected happiness: Nova Scotia was beautiful!

Mama gazed about too. "Samuel, isn't this the land the Acadians diked and drained?"

Papa answered slowly. "Yes."

"Then where are the ploughed fields with crops?"

"There was a terrible storm several years ago. It destroyed the dikes and the fields. No one's been able to repair and drain them."

They rounded a corner and Papa stopped talking. A lovely new house stood at the top of a hill, facing the bay. It was long and low with two dormer windows in the roof.

"Our new home, my dears," Papa said proudly.

Mama whispered, "It's a dream come true, Samuel!"

But Elizabeth couldn't speak. Between the new house and a barn stood another building: a small log cabin. Frozen with dread, she stared at its thatched roof. It was the little house from her nightmare.

Elizabeth slept poorly that first night in the cabin. The Worths and the Youngs were settled in to the new, big house. Elizabeth felt sure that until their houses were built and she could move out of the cabin, she wouldn't enjoy one good night's sleep.

Who would burn the little house down? A soldier? A ghost? Sarah Worth?

Late, late in the night she woke to a loud creak. She rose and scrambled over to a tiny window in the loft, surprised to see a rosy hint of dawn outside. The sound had come from the direction of the barn. Maybe Papa had started chores already. She dressed eagerly. She would gather eggs, milk Bessie, feed the animals, and talk with Papa. They had a farm again!

Elizabeth crept down the ladder to the main room below. In the dimness she saw Papa still asleep beside Mama in the strange bed built into the wall. Perplexed, she wondered what to do. Should she wake Papa? It wasn't something urgent. It was probably only the wind . . . or another dream? Better to light a lantern and check the barn herself.

She slipped outside quietly and hurried to the barn. With a push, the door creaked open. That same creak.

Elizabeth held the lantern high and headed into the long, trembling shadows. She shone the light into the pigs' and horses' stalls first.

"Who's there?"

The only answer was the sound of animals restless to start the day.

She scolded herself. What did she fear? An ambush of Acadians? Impossible! Yet the uneasy feeling wouldn't leave her. Something— someone—had woken her. Maybe it was a wanderer, some poor traveller who'd taken shelter in the barn overnight and slipped out before dawn.

She hung the lantern on a nail beside the hens and gathered her apron into a pouch to hold eggs for breakfast. To her dismay, there were none.

"What's wrong?" she scolded the hens. "You laid a dozen eggs on that miserable ship. You should lay two dozen now that you're home."

The hens clucked and rustled their feathers. Annoyed, Elizabeth clucked back.

She climbed into the cow's stall next. "Milking time, Bessie." She gave the tawny brown cow a big hug. "Maybe you'll tell me. Do *you* like your new home?"

Moooo.

Elizabeth laughed. "*Moooo* to you, too." She pushed a pail under Bessie's udder and sat on a short stool beside it. Leaning her forehead against Bessie's warm flank, she began to pull gently. Creamy milk began a rhythmic *squirt, squirt* into the pail.

But before long, Bessie bawled uncomfortably. The milk was tapering off to a dribble. Elizabeth stared at the tiny bit in the pail. "Where's your milk? What happened out here—"

Creak!

Elizabeth leapt off her stool, knocking over the pail. With her heart pounding, she turned to see a figure, shadowy in the doorway.

"Papa!" She ran and threw her arms around him.

"What's all this? Not still missing me, are you?" He tousled her hair.

"No, Papa. I mean . . . yes, but that's not it. There's something strange. Someone's been here. There are no eggs. No milk."

"There's never any milk when you knock over the pail." Papa laughed.

Elizabeth scrunched up her eyebrows. This was

not the right moment for teasing.

Papa placed a fingertip where her brows met. "Didn't I ever tell you about the worrywart whose eyebrows stuck together?"

Elizabeth pulled away.

"It's either a poor soul who took food and shelter for the night," he reassured her. "Or maybe the animals are overexcited now that you're finally here. Either way, it's nothing to worry about." Papa took the lantern off the nail. "Mama's got breakfast ready. Then, if you promise to smile, you can go into Fort Edward with me later."

In the bustle of eating and getting the carts hitched, Elizabeth managed to put the strange morning behind her. But when she and Papa were really ready to go, she saw Sarah Worth outside, and it all came back.

Sarah was waving goodbye to her father in his cart. Her curls were perfect, her dress new and clean. Elizabeth clambered into their cart beside Papa, trying to hide the dirty hem of her skirt.

"We're going to finish our samplers today," Sarah called out.

Elizabeth didn't answer. Was this Sarah's idea of an invitation? Or an accusation? Sarah was *so* annoying. Then Elizabeth remembered the barn. Maybe it was Sarah who took the eggs and milk.

"Don't forget to milk the cows," she called back, scrutinizing Sarah's face. She nearly added, ". . . *again.*"

Sarah wrinkled her nose with obvious distaste. "Milking cows is boys' work."

The cart rounded a sharp bend in the road. Sarah disappeared from view, but her remark buzzed around Elizabeth's thoughts like a pesky fly. She stared at the deep ruts in the road, and then she turned her head sharply to look at Papa.

"Do you think I should have been a boy?" she asked.

"No! I like you fine as a girl."

"But I don't like doing girl things."

"Hmm." Papa glanced at her thoughtfully and shifted in his seat. "Look at this road, Elizabeth. See what happens when the carts follow the exact same path? They dry into deep, rigid ruts that we get stuck in. If you ask me, we all travel the same road, but God meant us each to be a little different. You're a girl who likes doing boy things."

They jostled along in silence for a while. The wooden wheels creaked. The horses snorted. The air was sweet with the smells of early summer. Elizabeth slipped her arm through Papa's and felt much better. Along the shore the mud flats were criss-crossed with deep crevices. She imagined they'd be filled with shells and mussels clinging to rocks. Oh, to go exploring with Papa!

As soon as they pulled into the fort Elizabeth's warm, happy feeling disappeared. The Acadian children she'd seen yesterday were huddled in front of tents with their parents. Soldiers guarded them. Elizabeth hated the thought of a rifle pointed at *her*. A number of old people, probably grandparents, lay on the ground resting in the sun. Elizabeth wished she could come back with Mama and bring them comfortable bedding and hot soup. Then she noticed the girl with fierce dark eyes standing beside a man and woman. She was pointing right at Elizabeth, which made her flush bright red. Why would she point at her?

Papa reined in the horses and nodded at several men. The Planters were gathered in front of Caleb Worth and Captain Mercer. Caleb Worth stood on a box and nodded at Papa before he began to speak.

"Today," he announced, "we begin assembling the Porters' house. Emma Porter is expecting a baby any day and her needs are most urgent . . ."

Elizabeth groaned. Just this once, couldn't Caleb Worth put his own needs first?

He explained how they would proceed with

the reconstructions. Captain Mercer offered some soldiers to clear a field for them. "You Planters need to get planting," he said, pleased when the men chuckled.

"What about the marshlands?" asked Elizabeth's father.

"We don't have enough expertise or men to rebuild the dikes and drain the land . . . although there will be more soldiers available after the Acadians leave. I have received orders to send them to Halifax as soon as possible."

Elizabeth heard cries from the Acadians but was too scared to look.

Caleb Worth raised both hands. "May I suggest that we ask God's blessing as we undertake the building of our new homes and community?" All the men bowed their heads. Caleb began to pray.

Elizabeth closed her eyes but squirmed uncomfortably. The Acadians were awfully quiet behind them. She opened her eyes to peek.

All of them, even the girl, had bowed their heads too. How confusing! What could it mean?

Protestants and Catholics praying at the same time . . . surely not to the same God? Did they want the land back? Would God have to take sides? *What* were the Acadians praying for?

CHAPTER N° 5

Nova Scotia in the rain wasn't much different from Connecticut. Three mornings in a row, Elizabeth woke late. The sky was dark. Rain *shushed* steadily on the thatched roof.

Mama insisted that they join the other women at work in the new house. Mama laughed happily as she pounded bread and shaped pies with Rebecca Worth and Catherine Young. Elizabeth pouted as she peeled vegetables. She had to listen to Sarah read Bible verses, trying to pick one for Priscilla's sampler. Elizabeth nearly shouted for joy when the skies cleared and Mama allowed her to go outside.

Immediately, she ran to the barn. Would there be anything amiss today? Of course it couldn't have been Sarah Worth. Maybe it had been a ghost, a hungry Acadian ghost. It couldn't be real, *live* Acadians. They were prisoners and under guard in the fort.

But no one was in the barn, dead or alive. All the animals were safe and sound. There were plenty of eggs and lots of milk. Elizabeth began to wonder if Mama was right. Maybe strange feelings were strange feelings, and nothing more. Moving was an unsettling and anxious time.

Three afternoons in a row she dug the vegetable garden with Mama. Mama wasn't the least bit anxious. She glowed with happiness. "Once your garden's planted," she exclaimed, walking between rows of cabbages and carrots, "you know you're home."

"Can we plant something new? For our new home?" Elizabeth asked. Mama's good mood was infectious.

Mama looked thoughtful. "Rebecca Worth gave me pumpkin seeds. It's such a big garden. Maybe we could try some in a corner."

They were just turning the earth for the seeds when Sarah, Priscilla, and Maggie came outside.

"We're going to walk along the dike. Can you come?" asked Maggie.

Before she could say no, Mama answered, "Of course she can."

"No I can't. What about the pumpkins?"

Mama nudged her towards the girls. "Go with your friends while they're still here. They'll be moving soon."

Friends? Sarah Worth? She was going to the one place she was dying to explore with the one person she was dying to avoid. She dragged behind the girls down the road to the dike. Much to her dismay, Sarah positioned herself so that she was walking beside her.

"Why don't you wear shoes? Doesn't the ground hurt?"

Elizabeth looked at her dirty bare feet. She loved the feel of the earth—rough, soft, wet, or dry. Hard calluses protected her skin. If only she could get some to protect her from Sarah Worth.

"Don't you hate stockings?" she asked back.

"Not any more, though I did when I was younger. Do you still have your terrible feeling?"

Was Sarah's voice mocking? Elizabeth couldn't tell. Briefly, she considered turning back. But on one side of the dike the long grass danced in the wind, while on the other the tide was going out. Everything invited her to explore.

Sarah lowered her voice. "You were right, after all. What you said on the boat. It's those Acadians. Papa's giving Captain Mercer the *Lydia* to take them to Halifax. We'll all feel better once they're gone."

Better? Elizabeth could barely breathe she felt so horrified. She remembered the ragged families huddled outside the tents in Fort Edward. They were already worn-out and hungry. How would they survive the *Lydia?* It was dark, damp, filthy. Had Sarah forgotten?

"You haven't visited Fort Edward," Elizabeth cried angrily. "If you saw them you'd know there's nothing to fear. They're just families like us, only they're sick and . . ." she remembered the old people lying in the sun ". . . *tired*. They won't hurt anybody, I know it."

Priscilla took Sarah's side. "How do you know that? What if we feed them and they get better and want their land back?" Her voice squeaked with fear.

"I wish they'd go away," Maggie whimpered.

Elizabeth wanted to scream. "They need a home too," she choked out.

She felt angry and helpless at the same time. She'd never forget leaving home. Placing stones for the last time on her brothers' graves. And that hateful sea captain who bought their house. What if Nova Scotia didn't work out and they went back to Connecticut . . . and the sea captain ordered *them* away! With guns!

"Look!" Sarah interrupted, pointing at the water. The girls stopped arguing. A tall, white bird was poised on one long, black leg in the shallows, his other leg tucked under his snowy feathers.

"I've seen that bird before, back home."

Sarah's voice startled the bird. He spread his elegant wings and took off over the water, stretching both legs behind his body.

Sarah's words echoed in Elizabeth's head—*back home.*

Suddenly, Elizabeth took off too. Something about the bird called to her heart, tugged her down the slope of the dike.

She ran fast, holding her blue-and-white skirt high. Cold water splashed on her legs. Behind her, growing faint, she heard the girls calling, *"Wait, wait!"*

Tug, tug, tug, on her heart. *Catch up with the bird. Flying. Home.*

She couldn't wait. The bird was beautiful, its neck a graceful S against the clean blue sky. His white wings beat against the air. She could almost hear them, feel the brush of feathers on her cheek.

Why couldn't they all live here? It could be home to everyone. Elizabeth spread her skirt wide, closed her eyes, and pretended she was flying.

Sunday morning, light streamed in the little window under the thatched roof. The delicious smell of baking bread woke Elizabeth and she scrambled downstairs, eager to eat breakfast and explore her new world.

"Shhh," Mama whispered. "It's the Sabbath. The men worked late finishing the Worths' house. Papa's bone-tired. Let him sleep in until Meeting."

Elizabeth groaned. Why couldn't Meetings stay back in Connecticut? "Must we have Meeting?

There's no minister."

Mama scolded her. "I know what you're thinking, and *yes,* we must. Caleb Worth will lead the Meeting in our new house. And don't dare suggest you can't wear your good dress and stockings. I found them in the bottom of your trunk."

Elizabeth grabbed a slice of hot bread and slipped out the door, pretending she hadn't heard. "I have chores."

"You heard me, young lady," Mama called after her. "Stockings. And don't be late."

Elizabeth scowled and trudged out to the barn. There was no fathoming adults and their Meetings. She gave the animals fresh water and food, hugged Bessie, then sat down to milk her.

"You're lucky, Bessie," she said. "You don't have to sit through sermons and Rebecca Worth's singing." Elizabeth screeched, *"I know th-a-a-at my Redeemer liveth"* in a high voice, wobbling over the vowels. Bessie turned her head and bellowed a long and complaining *moooo.*

"No, not like that—"

Bessie bawled again.

Elizabeth stared into the empty pail. Oh no! Bessie was complaining for another reason. "You're out of milk again?" Elizabeth cried.

She ran over to the hens. Sure enough, there were no eggs.

Elizabeth searched the barn carefully. Empty.

"That's one greedy ghost," she muttered, "or rude, hungry travellers," she said to Bessie. "I wish you'd tell me what's going on." Perplexed, she left the barn shaking her head.

At Meeting, Elizabeth forgot about the missing food. Instead she played rhyming games in her head. *Boring, snoring, I'd rather be exploring.* Caleb Worth's prayers were unbearably long. The Bible reading had no story. This one begat that one, who could remember all those names? Then the worst: Rebecca Worth croaked like a lovesick frog through the hymns.

Afterwards, Elizabeth sat on the hallway stairs with six other girls. When the adults began discussing community plans, Rebecca Worth let the girls who had finished their samplers start making lace collars. Elizabeth was the only one still holding an unfinished sampler, and she stared at it gloomily.

"What's wrong?" Maggie whispered.

"I can't sew," she whispered back. "I'll never finish."

But she hadn't whispered quietly enough. Sarah Worth, sitting on the step below, turned around to stare, first at the sampler, then into Elizabeth's face.

Foo on you! Elizabeth thought.

Sarah opened her mouth like a fish, paused, and, amazingly, shut it without saying a word.

Just then Papa emerged from the company room. He nodded at Elizabeth. "Meeting's over. Mama's staying for the potluck, but," he winked, "we have something to do, right?"

Elizabeth dropped her sampler, climbed over Sarah Worth, and with a joyful "Excuse me!" escaped with Papa.

Once outside, she yanked his sleeve. "*What* do we have to do, Papa?"

"Dig for clams," he answered. "You can't wear your stockings—"

Elizabeth whooped and ran to get ready. In no time, they were walking barefoot on the dike in the sunshine. Elizabeth swung a wooden bucket in one hand and Papa's hand in the other.

"So, Elizabeth. How do you like being a Planter?" Papa asked. They were walking down the slope of the dike towards the beach where she'd run behind the snowy bird.

If Papa had asked her three months ago, she'd have shared her bad dream and worries. But right this minute, she was so filled with good feelings she forgot even the mystery in the barn.

"I like it," she chirped.

The wet sand was cool under her feet. Suddenly just ahead she saw water squirt from the ground. She ran up and started digging.

"Our first clam in Nova Scotia!" she shouted, pulling out a shell.

They walked for hours, scanning the exposed shore for bubbles, and pulled up a feast of clams, which they dropped with a clatter into the bucket.

When the bucket was brimming, Papa announced, "Tide's coming in. Let's go home."

They headed up the dike. Elizabeth noticed a tunnel through the hill and bent to stare into it.

"Look, Papa. A wooden door."

"That's one of the Acadian 'clappers.' They're mostly broken now. The Acadians had a clever system to keep the sea water off the fields at high tide." Papa sighed. "I'd give anything to get this land back the way the Acadians had it."

Off in the distance, Elizabeth could see their new house, with the old Acadian house and barn beside it. "Maybe some of the Acadians could stay and help you."

Papa stopped to stare thoughtfully at the expanse of marshland beside them.

"Your eyebrows are growing together," Elizabeth said.

Papa laughed. "I can't believe what you said."

"About your eyebrows?"

"No. About the Acadians. It's an interesting idea. Of course the others . . ." Papa combed his fingers through his brown hair, thinking out loud. "Caleb Worth might not go for it. Or Captain Mercer." He looked sharply at Elizabeth. "Even the Acadians. Hard to say how they might feel, repairing their former fields for English settlers."

Captain Mercer was shipping the Acadians to Halifax in two days. Elizabeth imagined the hungry, tired families huddled in a dark, dirty hold. She couldn't keep her worries to herself.

"It's got to be better than leaving on the *Lydia*," she said.

Terrified, Elizabeth woke up with a scream in her throat. It was the dream again . . . except this time, she was flying with the snowy bird over the fire. Flames devoured the house, the thatched roof . . . spreading from her skirt to the roof of the barn.

Wide awake, she ran to the little window. It was dark outside. She swallowed her scream and took a deep, calming breath.

Then she saw a flicker of light. It moved from the shadowy orchard . . . to the barn.

Creak.

Someone had entered the barn! With a lantern.

She scrambled down the ladder. Papa was snoring, sound asleep. She remembered Mama's words: "Papa's bone-tired." What if she was wrong again? It would be better not to wake him.

On the other hand, was the dream a warning? Maybe someone was setting the barn on fire right now!

Elizabeth ran outside. The ground was cool, wet with dew. Panting, she reached the barn door. What should she do? She should peek.

Creak!

She stared in amazement. There *was* someone in the barn. But it wasn't Sarah Worth, or a soldier, or a ghost, or a traveller. It was the girl with the black button eyes. And she was staring back at Elizabeth, her face white with terror.

The girl stood frozen, one hand under a hen in its nesting box, the other hand gathering her bulging apron. A lantern rested at her feet.

The girl stood frozen, one hand under a hen in its nesting box, the other hand gathering her bulging apron.

Suddenly she came to life. She yanked her hand away from the hen, but it pecked hard at her wrist. She screamed and let go of her apron. Eggs flew, cracking white and yellow on the ground. Her foot knocked over the lantern. Bright orange flames caught her hem and flashed across the girl's dress.

For one agonizing second Elizabeth had the bone-chilling sensation of being *in* her nightmare. The barn was going to burn down—starting with this girl!

Elizabeth flew into action. There was a bucket on the ground, full of milk. Half aware that it was probably Bessie's milk, she picked it up and threw it on the girl's skirts, dousing the fire. She dumped the empty bucket in Bessie's water trough and threw water on the last surrendering flames.

Then Elizabeth fell to her knees beside the girl. "Are you all right?"

The girl stared, stunned, at the black edge of her wet skirt, then at the eggs splattered around them.

She burst out sobbing, "Now there's nothing to eat." She glared at Elizabeth. "It's all your fault. You English want to kill us."

Elizabeth stammered, "What? Me? I just saved you."

"Saved me? All the eggs are broken. You threw the milk."

"You were on fire! You're lucky I came," Elizabeth cried. Why was this girl being this way? "Besides—it's not your food. You're stealing *our* food. And I bet it was you the other mornings, wasn't it? When it's not raining, you come from the fort to steal food from our barn."

"*Our* barn," the girl cried.

And then a terrible look came into her eyes. All of a sudden, her whole face changed. The fierceness disappeared. Her shoulders dropped. Tears streamed down her cheeks.

"*Our* food," she said, her voice trembling. "*Our* land." She hid her face in her hands. "You English stole everything."

The girl's words cut right into Elizabeth's

heart. But just because she spoke English, that didn't mean she had stolen their lands. England controlled Nova Scotia.

"We're Planters from Connecticut. We aren't stealing," she whispered back. "The English invited us here. We're trying to make a new home."

The girl lifted her head. Her eyes were defiant again, though still teary. "And we're trying to come home."

Bessie bawled. Elizabeth was at a loss for words. What could she say to this girl? She didn't even know her name.

"My name's Elizabeth Brightman. What's yours?"

The girl seemed to think this over. "Mathilde LeBlanc," she said.

"You speak English perfectly."

"I learned in Massachusetts, working in English homes."

"Your skirt's burned. I'll get you one of mine. We're about the same size."

The girl didn't say anything.

"And some cheese and bread."

Hunger showed on the girl's face. "There's little to eat at the fort. The old and the young are always sick."

"Stay here. I'll bring food."

"You mustn't tell anyone. I don't know what Captain Mercer would do."

"I promise I won't tell."

The girl nodded.

Elizabeth ran back to the house. Mama and Papa were eating breakfast.

Thinking quickly, she said, "I'm going with the girls for a picnic on the dikes for our last morning together. May I pack a basket?"

Mama's face lit with pleasure. "What a wonderful idea. I'm so glad you're getting along. Pack whatever you need."

Elizabeth hated lying. Then she remembered the children and the old people, all too thin. The girl was right. It wasn't *exactly* stealing.

Mama and Papa kept talking. It was moving

day—houses had at last been built for the Worths and Youngs—and they were excited about setting up in their new home at last. Elizabeth stuffed fruit and jam under the cheese and bread and ran back to the barn with a loaded basket.

"Mathilde?" she called, trying to pronounce it the way the girl had.

The hens clucked quietly in their corner. Bessie stared at her, twitching her ears. Elizabeth dropped the basket and scrambled through the barn, frantically searching every stall. Once again, the barn was empty.

CHAPTER N°· 8

Elizabeth couldn't seem to find the right opportunity to speak with Papa. Had he spoken to Caleb Worth? All morning they were busy moving the Youngs out. At noon they feasted on clams together. In the afternoon they began to pack up the Worths. There was never a quiet moment to ask Papa about the Acadians.

The Worths had so many belongings that they needed to borrow Papa's cart, too. As Elizabeth carried blankets and pots in and out of her new house, she felt a growing excitement. This was her new home. It was big and bright with an inviting view of the bay.

For some strange reason, Sarah Worth stared at her whenever they passed on the stairs. Elizabeth had a strong feeling that she wanted to talk, but she avoided her, praying silently: *Maybe the Worths could move to the other side of Nova Scotia?*

Elizabeth paused in her new room to look out the window. White clouds puffed past the sun, and their shadows sailed like ships across the Minas Basin below . . . and that reminded her. The Acadians would be on the *Lydia* tomorrow. She *had* to make Papa do something. Time was running out.

She heard footsteps behind her and a heavy thud. Sarah and her father stood in the doorway with Elizabeth's trunk. They pushed it up against the foot of her bed. Then Caleb Worth left the room, and suddenly Elizabeth was alone with Sarah Worth.

"I wanted to thank you for your hospitality," Sarah said. "I . . . we . . . it would have been awful to stay at the fort."

Elizabeth folded her arms over her chest. "You mean with the Acadians?"

"Yes."

"You think they're awful people?"

"I never said that. You twisted my words. You don't really like me, do you?"

What? Why would Sarah care if she liked her? "I just think you're not giving the Acadians a chance."

"What kind of chance? They're prisoners in Fort Edward. The English rule this land, Elizabeth Brightman. The English are deporting them, not me!"

"Your father's an elder. He owns the *Lydia*. Captain Mercer might listen to him. Those families are starving so badly there's—" She nearly blurted out that there was a girl stealing food, a girl just like them, only homeless and hungry. Elizabeth kicked her trunk in frustration. "Forget it. You'd never understand."

Sarah's eyes shone with tears. "I'm not the ogre

you think I am. I'm not!" she cried, and she ran from the room.

Well! This was a day of surprises. Elizabeth shook her head. She'd never called Sarah an ogre.

Slowly, she walked downstairs, then outside, just in time to see Sarah leave with her parents.

Twice in one day—two girls had run away from her.

Papa was in his cart just about to leave too. What if he hadn't spoken to Caleb Worth?

A bucket of clam shells stood by her feet. Frantic, she picked one out and hurled it at the cart.

Whack—it hit one of the horses, causing it to rear up. Papa half stood, reining the team in sharply, calling, "Steady, steady." The cart wheeled around in a crazy circle before the horses snorted, pranced a little and were finally calm.

Papa stared at Elizabeth in disbelief. "Did you throw something?"

Elizabeth trembled. How could she explain?

"What's happening to the Acadians?" she asked.

"What do you mean? They're being deported tomorrow."

"But, Papa. You said you'd ask if some could stay."

"I didn't."

"You did! Yesterday, remember?" Her voice cracked. "You were going to ask Caleb Worth and Captain Mercer if any Acadians could work on the dikes. Then they wouldn't be deported again."

Papa looked at her long and hard. "In some families, children are expected to be seen and not heard, to obey and not question." He was angrier than she'd ever seen him. "They are certainly not expected to start a stampede!"

He paused, looking towards heaven.

"Thankfully, God didn't grace me with such a child."

Papa repositioned his hat on his head. "All right, Elizabeth. We'll try to help the Acadians. But I warn you, many Congregationalists fear them, and *you,* young lady, must respect that. The

English consider the Acadians to be French enemies. But if Caleb Worth and Captain Mercer agree, we'll offer them work tomorrow before they load the ship. They'll probably leave at high tide in the afternoon. It's not in our hands, Elizabeth. Do you understand that?"

Elizabeth nodded. She'd never argued with Papa, ever. Her hands were shaking and she gripped them tightly.

Papa's cart disappeared around the bend, throwing up dust behind it.

Please God, she prayed. *Open their hearts. Let them say yes.*

Head down, she walked inside, up the stairs, and into her room. She needed to think. Was she right to trust her strong feeling? The Acadians didn't look like enemies. They looked like them, like Planters, only homeless.

She knelt beside her trunk. She had a new home. Should she unpack? She lifted the lid and looked inside. On top of her few belongings was something strange. She gasped.

It was her sampler—*finished*. It was framed in wood, the corners neatly dovetailed together. Above her alphabet someone had cross-stitched a brown house with dormers—her house. Over it flew a snowy white bird in a blue sky. Its wings looked amazingly like Elizabeth's skirt.

At the top, stitched in indigo to match the alphabet, were three simple words:

Bless This House

Sarah Worth must have found her sampler yesterday, finished it, and asked her father to frame it. It was beautiful.

Elizabeth burned with shame. Who had been the ogre? Who needed to open her heart? In her sampler she read another message, three invisible words stitched with the thread of kindness: *Be my friend*.

CHAPTER Nº 9

Elizabeth woke with the first light of dawn.
She dressed as fast as her fingers would allow and
ran to the barn.

Please, Mathilde, be there.

The barn was empty. Her heart sank with
disappointment.

Slowly she milked Bessie . . . a full pail of milk.
Then she gathered two dozen eggs. Mathilde
hadn't come. It didn't make sense. Today of all
days, she should have come. She would need
food for the voyage. Something was wrong.

As she walked back to the house, the rising sun began to shed light on the day. Elizabeth looked at the bay. It was high tide. What if they were leaving now and not waiting till late afternoon? There wasn't a minute to lose. She ran to the house.

"Papa!" She shook him awake. "She didn't come. There's eggs and milk." Her words got jumbled in her hurry. "The fire was a warning. I think they're leaving. We have to go now!"

Papa sat up groggily, shaking the sleep from his head. "You're not making sense. What girl? What fire?"

"Please, Papa! It's high tide. They're not leaving this afternoon. I think the *Lydia*'s leaving now. Please, please can we go?"

"All right. Calm down. I'll get the cart hitched. We'll go."

Quickly Elizabeth packed eggs and all the food she could find into a basket and joined her father in the cart. Her panic spread to the horses, into their pounding hooves. *Hurry-up, hurry-up.*

Elizabeth pointed ahead. In the distance, they saw people moving from the fort to the wharf where the *Lydia* waited.

Papa drove faster than he'd ever driven before. They wheeled in, pulling in beside another cart. What a shock to see Sarah Worth sitting in that cart while her father unloaded sacks from it onto the ground.

The Acadians stood on the dock in family groupings, arms around one another. Elizabeth scanned the crowd. Mathilde stood beside a man and woman, and several older boys. They had no luggage or trunks, just a few baskets.

Papa jumped from their cart. "Don't move. I'll speak with Caleb Worth and Captain Mercer."

Caleb Worth was ordering two seamen to load the sacks of flour, oats, and sugar onto the ship.

"What are you doing with your provisions, Caleb?"

Caleb grumbled. "I'll get no peace from my daughter if I don't share some of our food with the Acadian prisoners."

Elizabeth stared at Sarah in surprise. She nearly jumped out of the cart to hug her.

Papa nodded. "And I'll get no peace from mine if I don't have a word with you and Captain Mercer. Could we, Caleb?"

The two men walked towards the wharf, heads bent in discussion. At one point, Caleb shook his head vehemently. Elizabeth's heart pounded. But Papa kept talking, gesturing with his hands, until they joined up with Captain Mercer and the whole thing started again: heads bent, heads shook, Papa gestured with his hands.

Sarah asked, "What does your father want?"

"Papa wants to rebuild his marsh lot. He wonders if any Acadians might stay and work."

Sarah's smile disappeared. She tightened her shawl protectively around her. "He'd trust them?"

Elizabeth reminded herself how long it had taken her to see Sarah's good qualities. Sarah needed time to see the Acadians differently.

"Look at them, Sarah." The Acadians were

crossing themselves as they prayed.

"I am looking. They're Catholics, Elizabeth. *French Catholics!*"

"You brought French Catholics food."

Sarah rolled her eyes, then smiled reluctantly. "It seemed a good idea, though Papa thought it . . . *unusual.*" Something flashed in her eyes. "Where do you get *your* unusual ideas?"

Was that envy in Sarah's voice?

"Where did you get the idea to finish my sampler?"

"Do you like it?" Elizabeth heard the unmistakeable hope in Sarah's voice.

"It's beautiful, though Mama and Papa guessed I was responsible for the alphabet."

Just then, Captain Mercer called for attention.

"I have an extraordinary announcement. One of the Planters is eager to rebuild his marsh lot. If there be a family amongst you willing to work in return for food and lodging, let them step forward now. You will, of course, remain prisoners of his Majesty, George the Third, and subject to my orders."

There were murmurs among the families. None came forward. Disappointed, Elizabeth watched as Mathilde spoke to the man beside her, pointing at Elizabeth, then Papa. The man spoke to the woman and three teenaged boys behind them.

He shook his head at Mathilde. Her face turned to stone.

Inside Elizabeth something rose with the force of a tide. She couldn't sit here and do nothing, no matter what Papa had ordered.

She leapt from the cart, grabbed the basket of food and pushed her way forward to stand in front of Mathilde.

"Please. Take it. Share it. The voyage is so terrible . . ."

Mathilde looked at the basket. Eggs showed on top.

Again she turned to the man and woman beside her, her face alive with emotion. She began to cry. The woman did too. The man put

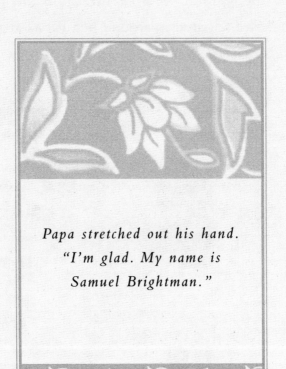

Papa stretched out his hand.
"I'm glad. My name is
Samuel Brightman."

his arms around them both and they whispered together.

Elizabeth trembled. Had she done the right thing? She felt an arm around her, Papa's arm.

Finally the man turned to face Papa and Elizabeth. "My girls say we rest here. We stay," he said, with a heavy French accent.

Papa stretched out his hand. "I'm glad. My name is Samuel Brightman."

The Acadian shook Papa's hand. "Joseph LeBlanc." He looked at Elizabeth and a smile danced in his black eyes. "It seems in these difficult times that God talks only to girls. *Dieu merci*, at least these girls listen to someone."

CHAPTER N.º 10

They drove home in silence. Mathilde and her family took their few belongings from the cart and stood awkwardly, as if awaiting orders.

Papa spoke kindly. "The little house is yours for as long as the English let you stay. That's our house beside yours. We're neighbours. Please . . ." He pointed to the log house with the thatched roof.

At this, Mathilde's mother brought her hands to her face and began to sob. Her husband and sons gathered around her and led her slowly towards the little house.

Mathilde stayed behind. There was a long silence. With her toes, she traced a slow circle in the ground as if searching for the right words to say.

"It was our house."

She looked directly at Elizabeth.

At first Elizabeth didn't understand her meaning.

"I tried to tell you. All these weeks, I've been coming here. The soldiers don't care about a girl running in the forest in the early morning. Like a horse, my feet remembered the way home."

Home. Elizabeth could scarcely believe it. This was actually the LeBlancs' house and barn?

Mathilde continued. "Most of the other homes, the English burned. They burned them before our eyes. For miles and miles, up and down the Basin, the sky was black with smoke." Mathilde's black eyes grew shiny with remembering.

Could it be? She'd seen the Acadian houses burning in her dreams?

"Except our home and a few others. It's a miracle. Mama says it has to mean something, us coming back and finding our house still standing, don't you think?"

Elizabeth nodded silently, too awed to speak. She looked out towards the bay. Gulls circled and dove for food. Along the shore, the marsh grasses reflected gold in the morning sun. If the marsh-land could change into rich fields of wheat and oats, maybe the Planters' fears about the Acadians could change too.

She smiled at Mathilde. "I'm glad you're staying. Would you like to go exploring with me sometime?"

Mathilde looked thoughtful. "Our favourite place used to be Pirate Island. I'm sure I remember the way."

Elizabeth's eyes lit up at the thought. Some of the other girls might like to come too.

Suddenly she hoped the Worths hadn't moved far away. *Please, God. I didn't really mean to the other side of Nova Scotia.* Something told her that Sarah didn't really want to be a twelve-year-old grand-mother. It was easy to imagine the three of them running barefoot on the beach, flying behind the great white bird.

Sometime soon, she hoped. Maybe tomorrow?

ACKNOWLEDGEMENTS

Thanks to Leona Trainer, my agent, and Donna Doucet and Margaret Conrad, historians in Nova Scotia.

Dear Reader,

Did you enjoy reading this Our Canadian Girl adventure? Write us and tell us what you think! We'd love to hear about your favourite parts, which characters you like best, and even whom else you'd like to see stories about. Maybe you'd like to read an adventure with one of Our Canadian Girls that happened in your hometown—fifty, a hundred years ago or more!

Send your letters to:
> Our Canadian Girl
> c/o Penguin Canada
> 10 Alcorn Avenue, Suite 300
> Toronto, ON M4V 3B2

Be sure to check your bookstore for more books in the Our Canadian Girl series. There are some ready for you right now, and more are on their way.

We look forward to hearing from you!

Sincerely,
> Barbara Berson
> PENGUIN BOOKS CANADA

P.S. Don't forget to visit us online at www.ourcanadiangirl.ca—there are some other girls you should meet!

1608
Samuel de
Champlain
establishes
the first
fortified
trading post
at Quebec.

1759
The British
defeat the
French in
the Battle
of the
Plains of
Abraham.

1812
The United
States
declares war
against
Canada.

1845
The expedition of
Sir John Franklin
to the Arctic ends
when the ship is
frozen in the pack
ice; the fate of its
crew remains a
mystery.

1869
Louis Riel
leads his
Métis
followers in
the Red
River
Rebellion.

1871
British
Columbia
joins
Canada.

1755
The British
expel the
entire French
population
of Acadia
(today's
Maritime
provinces),
sending
them into
exile.

1776
The 13
Colonies
revolt
against
Britain, and
the Loyalists
flee to
Canada.

1762
Elizabeth

1837
Calling for
responsible
government, the
Patriotes, following
Louis-Joseph
Papineau, rebel in
Lower Canada;
William Lyon
Mackenzie leads the
uprising in Upper
Canada.

1867
New
Brunswick,
Nova Scotia
and the United
Province of
Canada come
together in
Confederation
to form the
Dominion of
Canada.

1870
Manitoba joins
Canada. The
Northwest
Territories
become an
official
territory of
Canada.

Timeline

1885
At Craigellachie, British Columbia, the last spike is driven to complete the building of the Canadian Pacific Railway.

1898
The Yukon Territory becomes an official territory of Canada.

1914
Britain declares war on Germany, and Canada, because of its ties to Britain, is at war too.

1918
As a result of the Wartime Elections Act, the women of Canada are given the right to vote in federal elections.

1945
World War II ends conclusively with the dropping of atomic bombs on Hiroshima and Nagasaki.

1873
Prince Edward Island joins Canada.

1896
Gold is discovered on Bonanza Creek, a tributary of the Klondike River.

1905
Alberta and Saskatchewan join Canada.

1917
In the Halifax harbour, two ships collide, causing an explosion that leaves more than 1,600 dead and 9,000 injured.

1939
Canada declares war on Germany seven days after war is declared by Britain and France.

1949
Newfoundland, under the leadership of Joey Smallwood, joins Canada.

1896
Emily

1885
Marie-Claire

1917
Penelope

Don't miss your chance to meet all the girls in the Our Canadian Girl series...

The story takes place in Montreal during the smallpox epidemic of 1885. Marie-Claire, who lives in a humble home with her working-class family, must struggle to persevere through the illness of her cousin Lucille and the work-related injury of her father – even to endure the death of a loved one. All the while, Marie-Claire holds out hope for the future.

The year is 1917. Penny and her little sisters, Emily and Maggie, live with their father in a small house in Halifax. On the morning of December 6, Penny's father is at work, leaving Penny to get her sisters ready for the day. It is then that a catastrophic explosion rocks Halifax.

Ten-year-old Rachel arrives in northern Nova Scotia in 1783 with her mother, where they reunite with Rachel's stepfather after escaping slavery in South Carolina. Their joy at gaining freedom in a safe new home is dashed when they arrive, for the land they are given is barren and they don't have enough to eat. How will they survive?

Don't miss your chance to meet all the girls in the Our Canadian Girl series...

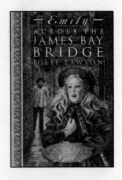

It's 1896 and Emily lives a middle-class life in Victoria, B.C., with her parents and two little sisters. She becomes friends with Hing, the family's Chinese servant and, through that relationship, discovers the secret world of Victoria's Chinatown.

It's 1939 and times are tough in Vancouver. Ellen's dad has just lost his job, and Ellen and her family have to move across town to stay with her grandfather. Ellen feels so lonely in her new home, and the neighbourhood around her feels unfamiliar. It is not until Ellen meets a new friend and discovers there are people who are much worse off than her that she will learn the true meaning of generosity.

Watch for more Canadian girls coming soon...